Published by Inhabit Media Inc.
www.inhabitmedia.com

Inhabit Media Inc. (Iqaluit) P.O. Box 11125, Iqaluit, Nunavut, X0A 1H0
(Toronto) 191 Eglinton Avenue East, Suite 301, Toronto, M4P 1K1

Edited by Neil Christopher and Kelly Ward
Art direction by Danny Christopher

This project was made possible in part by the Government of Canada.

We acknowledge the support of the Canada Council for the Arts for our publishing program.

Printed in Canada

ISBN: 978-1-77227-123-2

Library and Archives Canada Cataloguing in Publication

Webster, Deborah Kigjugalik, author
    Akilak's adventure / by Deborah Kigjugalik Webster
; illustrated by Charlene Chua.

ISBN 978-1-77227-123-2 (hardback)

    I. Chua, Charlene, 1980-, illustrator II. Title.

PS8645.E253A517 2016   jC813'.6   C2016-906154-X

Akilak's Adventure

by Deborah Kigjugalik Webster
illustrated by Charlene Chua

Not so long ago, when Inuit lived a traditional, nomadic life on the barren lands of the Arctic, there lived a young girl named Akilak. Akilak's mother had died when she was a baby, so her grandmother had adopted her. Akilak and her grandmother lived all alone on the land and rarely saw other people.

One morning, as they were preparing to go on a hunting trip, Akilak's grandmother sprained her ankle. Akilak watched as her grandmother carried on, limping and in pain. Eventually Akilak's grandmother said, "You must walk to your uncle's camp to get some food and bring it back. My foot hurts, so I have to stay here."

"I remember the way to the camp," Akilak said, knowing that their food supply was running low. "I can get the food."

Akilak's grandmother told her which route to take and assured her, "If you walk north at a good pace, you will reach the camp by nightfall." Akilak's eyes widened. She had never walked such a great distance before and felt uneasy about being on her own. Her grandmother raised her eyebrows in agreement. "Yes, granddaughter, you will walk a great distance, but keep in mind, *your destination is not running away; it will be reached eventually.*"

Carrying only a small amount of dry meat as a snack, Akilak set off toward her uncle's camp. She walked and walked. And as she walked, she thought about how wonderful it would be to see and play with her cousin again.

And she also thought about all the steps she would have to take to reach the camp before nightfall.

After what seemed like a long time, Akilak reached a stream with a large boulder beside it. She decided to have a snack and a drink of water from the cool stream. She unwrapped the dried meat and was about to take a big bite, when she suddenly saw a young, female caribou standing before her, grazing on lichen. The caribou lifted its head and stared at Akilak, but for some reason it did not run away.

Finally the caribou smiled and said, "You need not be afraid of me. I am harmless, really. I thought you might like some company on your journey. Have you much farther to go?"

"Oh, Caribou!" exclaimed Akilak. "You startled me. I thought I was all alone out here. Yes, I do have much father to go. It seems like an endless journey to my uncle's camp."

Although Caribou was a stranger, she seemed like a friendly animal and Akilak liked the idea of having a travelling companion, so she agreed to let Caribou walk with her.

After they had walked a while, Akilak sighed. "I have been walking north on this bumpy tundra for a long time, but it still seems I am no closer to my destination than when I started," she said.

"I understand how you feel," said Caribou. "When I go on a long journey, a migration, I sometimes feel the same way."

Akilak smiled. There was one question she could not resist asking. "Why are you not with the other caribou?"

"Well," said Caribou, "soon it will be time to migrate south to the treeline for the winter. I will be walking a great distance with many, many other caribou, but before I begin that journey, I would like some time on my own to explore. I am on an adventure!"

Akilak and Caribou reached a long lake and Akilak felt she was finally making progress. "Most evenings, after my grandmother has lit the oil lamp and we have settled down for bed, she tells me stories," Akilak told Caribou. "She tells me stories about people turning into animals and animals turning into people."

Akilak turned to look at Caribou's furry face and saw her raise her eyebrows in agreement.

"Yes, I know those stories," said Caribou with a knowing smile.

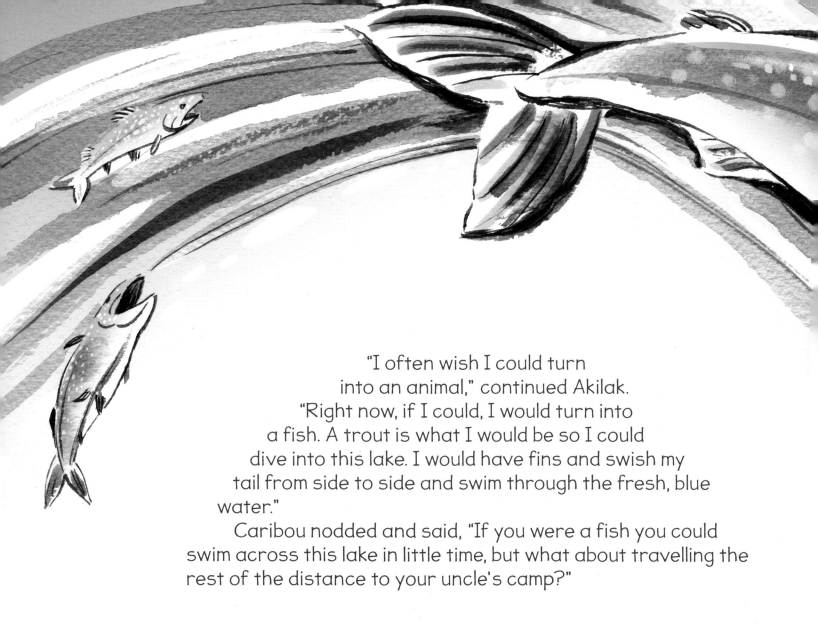

"I often wish I could turn
into an animal," continued Akilak.
"Right now, if I could, I would turn into
a fish. A trout is what I would be so I could
dive into this lake. I would have fins and swish my
tail from side to side and swim through the fresh, blue
water."

Caribou nodded and said, "If you were a fish you could
swim across this lake in little time, but what about travelling the
rest of the distance to your uncle's camp?"

"Well . . ." Akilak thought, looking down at the colourful tundra. "I would grow legs and turn into a wolf. With four legs I would be such a fast runner," said Akilak, as she imagined herself as a wolf bounding across the tundra.

Side by side, Akilak and Caribou continued walking. As they walked through a meadow, a cool breeze brushed Akilak's face. "Better still," Akilak said excitedly, "I would turn into a bird . . . geese are my favourite friends. My arms would turn into wings so I could fly." Lifting her arms up and down like a goose in flight she said, "I would flap my wings and feel the wind in my feathers. I would reach the camp very, very quickly! And I would not have to take another step!"

They both laughed. "You have quite the imagination, Akilak," said Caribou as she chuckled. Then she asked, "Do you really wish you were an animal instead of a person?"

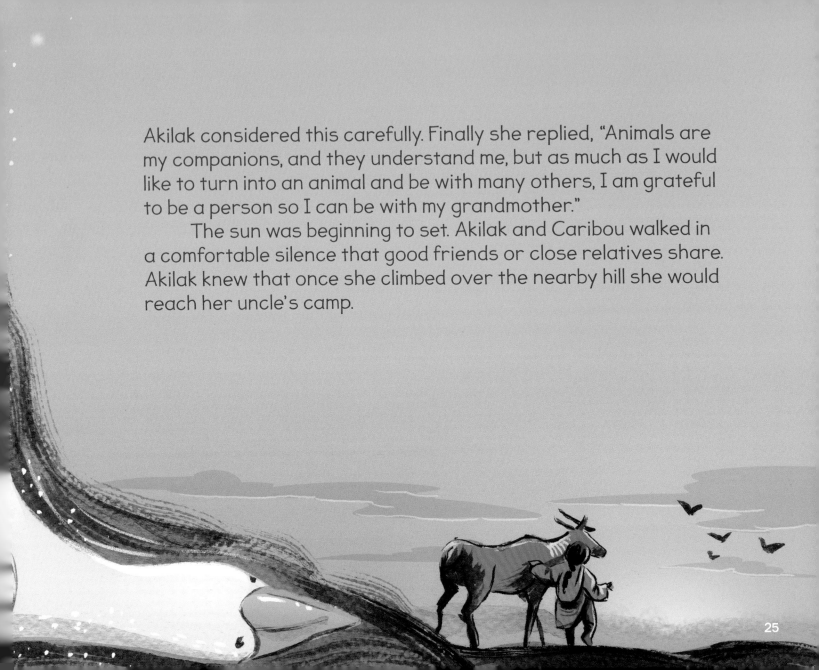

Akilak considered this carefully. Finally she replied, "Animals are my companions, and they understand me, but as much as I would like to turn into an animal and be with many others, I am grateful to be a person so I can be with my grandmother."

The sun was beginning to set. Akilak and Caribou walked in a comfortable silence that good friends or close relatives share. Akilak knew that once she climbed over the nearby hill she would reach her uncle's camp.

Caribou raised her head, sniffing the air, and said, "I have to go back now. I so enjoyed your stories."

"We made it here before dark," said Akilak, very pleased with herself. "I thought I would have to walk forever, Caribou, but with your company, my long journey did not seem to take so long after all!"

Caribou looked at Akilak and said with a smile, *"Your destination did not run away; you will reach it soon."*

Amazed that Caribou knew what her grandmother had told her, Akilak turned and asked, "How did you know that?"

But just as suddenly as Caribou had appeared, she was gone.

Although her new friend Caribou had left, and Akilak walked alone, there was a lightness in her step as she climbed to the top of the hill. There she looked around and saw the tents of her uncle's camp and her cousin waving and running toward her. Akilak smiled as she waved back. She had so much to tell about her journey. *No,* she thought, *I have so much to tell about my adventure!*

Deborah Kigjugalik Webster grew up in Baker Lake, Nunavut, where she loved to learn about her Inuit culture and heritage. She has a degree in Anthropology from Carleton University in Ottawa, Ontario, and works as an Inuit heritage researcher and author. The lack of published children's literature featuring Inuit content compelled Deborah to write this story for her daughters Sonja Akilak and Nicole Amaruq. Reading and making up stories with her daughters when they were young was a magical time in Deborah's life, and she took inspiration from their vivid imaginations and sense of wonderment and excitement. It is Deborah's hope that children and adults of all cultures will enjoy *Akilak's Adventure*.

Charlene Chua worked as a web designer, senior graphic designer, web producer, and interactive project manager before she decided to pursue illustration as a career. Her work has appeared in *American Illustration*, *Spectrum*, and SILA's *Illustration West*, as well as several art books. She illustrated the children's picture books *Julie Black Belt: The Kung Fu Chronicles* and *Julie Black Belt: The Belt of Fire*. She lives in Toronto.

Afterword

Akilak's Adventure is a fictional story set in a time in the not-so-distant past and in a place now called Nunavut. Within our elders' lifetime, the Inuit lifestyle has changed a great deal, but our culture holds strong and continues to be passed down from generation to generation.

Inuit ideas about travelling and mindset make up this story. The Inuit word *taulittuq* means "the experience of moving but without the sense of nearing one's destination." Perhaps Akilak experienced taulittuq when she travelled, but as her perspective changed, her long journey became an adventure!

The author's friend Peter Irniq said that his father, Athanasie Angutitaq, taught him an Inuktitut expression used when travelling on the land. Angutitaq would say, "*Qimaanngi'nami tikittumaakharaaluk!*" meaning "It is not running away; it will be reached—eventually."

INHABIT
MEDIA

Iqaluit • Toronto